Teasers from
A Pocketful of Riddles

Where does Friday come before Thursday?
Turn to page 20

What bites but has no teeth?
Turn to page 36

How can your pocket be empty
and still have something in it?
Turn to page 62

What has arms and legs but no head?

Turn to page 77

A POCKETFUL OF RIDDLES

DUTTON

Anytime

BOOKS

A Pocketful of
Riddles

Collected and Illustrated by

WILLIAM WIESNER

NEW YORK: E. P. DUTTON & CO., INC.

This Anytime Book edition first published in 1977
by E. P. Dutton & Co., Inc., New York

Published simultaneously in Canada by Clarke,
Irwin & Company Limited, Toronto and Vancouver

SBN: 0-525-45032-7   LCC: 66-11389

Printed in the U.S.A.
10   9   8   7   6   5   4   3   2   1

To all girls and boys

Which two letters of the alphabet
do children like best?

What letter do people drink?

C and Y   (candy).

T   (tea).

How many soft-boiled eggs could
the giant Goliath eat upon an
empty stomach?

*One — after which his
stomach was not empty.*

I go out every day,
still never leave
my home.

What am I?

A snail.

Although I am lying
on my belly, I run as
fast as the wind.

What am I?

Sailboat.

I have no feet,
yet I go to and fro.

What am I?

A saw.

The more you take away
from me, the bigger
I become.

    What am I?

A hole.

What kin is that child
to its father who is not
its father's own son?

His daughter.

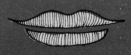

Which flowers do you
wear all year round?

Tulips   (two lips).

What travels around
the earth without
rockets?

The moon.

How many months
have thirty days?

Eleven!
(February
has 29.)

What is the most
difficult key to turn?

A don—key.

What is it that a clown keeps, even
when chased by an escaped lion?

TURN PAGE

His smile.

14

A DOWN-AND-UP VALENTINE

Read see how me
Down will I love
And you love you
Up and you if

Read down and up
and you will see
How I love you
If you love me.

Spell "hard water" with three letters.

What's in the middle
of Massachusetts?

The letter H.

Is it better to write
a letter on an empty
stomach or on a full
stomach?

*It is better
to write it on
paper.*

What is the end
of everything?

The letter G.

Can you jump higher
than a thirty-foot
wall?

Yes!

*(A wall can't
jump.)*

18

What is brought to
the table and cut,
but never eaten?

A pack of cards.

What goes all
the way from one
state to another
without moving
an inch?

The highway.

What fishes have
their eyes nearest
together?

The smallest.

19

Where does Friday come
before Thursday?

*In the
dictionary.*

Why does a donkey go
over the mountain?

*Because it can't
go under it.*

What bus crossed
the ocean?

Colum—bus.

What is it that is under a sunny sky
but cannot sun itself?

TURN PAGE

Your shadow.

22

What makes more noise
than a pig stuck
in a fence?

Two pigs.

What rooms can't
you enter?

Mush—rooms.

When do giraffes have
eight feet?

*When there are
two of them.*

23

Higher than a house,
Higher than a tree,
Oh, whatever can it be?

~~~~~~

Two brothers we are,
Great burdens we bear
By which we are bitterly pressed;
The truth is to say
We are full all the day
And empty when we go to rest.

A star.

A pair of shoes.

I see you are too wise for me.

With which hand should you
stir your cocoa?

With neither!
Stir it with your spoon.

Add five more lines to
these six to make
NINE.

What looks worse on your foot
than a darned sock?

TURN PAGE

One that needs darning.

The more it gets, the more it eats,
and when it has eaten everything,
it must die.

What is it?

Fire.

What animal are you
when you have a cold?

Horse   (hoarse).

What state of the
U.S.A. is high in
the middle and round
on both ends?

What is it that
everyone in the
world is doing
at the same time?

Growing older.

When do 2 and 2
make more than 4?

22

When they make 22.

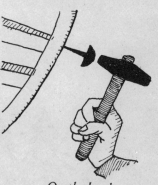

Where did Noah strike
the first nail he put
in the ark?

On the head.

13

When the clock
strikes 13, what
time is it?

*Time to have
the clock repaired.*

33

At what time of his life did
Paul Bunyan weigh the most?

When he was the heaviest.

35

Two boys and a girl are under one umbrella but none of them get wet. Why not?

It isn't raining.

When is a donkey spelled with one letter?

When it is U (you).

What bites but has no teeth?

Frost.

When the rain comes down,
what goes up?

TURN PAGE

Umbrellas.

One cannot eat a pie
and have it.

What goes around
a tree?

The bark.

What is the end
of the world?

The letter D.

Why do you go to bed
every night?

*Because the bed
won't come to you.*

When a boy falls into the water,
what is the first thing he does?

TURN PAGE

41

He gets wet.

MAGIC NUMBER

Add me to B
and I feel hurt.
Add me to E
and I *was* a dessert.

    What number am I?

B ten.

10

E ten.

43

What has eyes
but cannot see?

A potato.

When is a river like
the letter T?

*When it must
be crossed.*

Two fathers and two
sons have shot three
rabbits. Yet each of
them has only one
rabbit. Why?

*They are grand-
father, father,
and son.*

What kind of stones
do you generally see
in the Colorado River?

Wet ones.

What's the difference
between an old dime
and a new nickel?

Five cents.

What driver never
gets arrested?

A screw—driver.

B🏐 *is*

t🎩 *ends*

All is well that ends well.

What are the biggest ants
in the world?

TURN PAGE

47

The gi—ants.

What smells most
in a drugstore?

The nose.

It is the child of my
parents, but neither
my brother, nor my
sister. What is it?

Myself.

My roots are above
and I grow downward.

What am I?

An icicle.

Why are some children like flannel?

*Because they shrink
from washing.*

What would happen if your aunt swallowed her teaspoon?

She wouldn't be able to stir.

What is light as a feather but even the strongest man can't hold it longer than sixty seconds?

His breath.

What is the keynote of good manners?

B natural.

One bird in the hand is
worth two in the bush.

ABOUT MISSES:

What miss is an error?

Mistake.

What miss needs a
solution?

Mystery.

What miss is sent out
by the church?

Missionary.

54

No smoke without fire.

As I was going to St. Ives
I chanced to meet nine old wives;
Each wife had nine sacks,
Each sack had nine cats,
Each cat had nine kitts.
Kitts, cats, sacks and wives,
How many were going to St. Ives?

YOU CAN NOT SEE THE CATS AND KITTENS
BECAUSE THEY ARE <u>IN</u> THE SACKS.

*Only myself. The old wives were
going in the opposite direction.*

How can you spell
dried grass with
just three letters?

Hay.

What has eyes and
sees not, ears and
hears not, a nose
and smells not?

A portrait.

Why do birds fly south
for the winter?

*Because they
cannot walk.*

How can you tell when an artist
is unhappy?

TURN PAGE

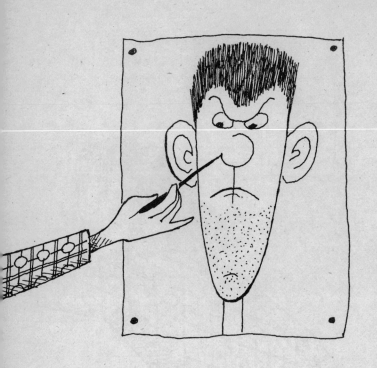

When he draws a long face.

Time is money.

What kind of coat
can be put on well
only when wet?

A coat of paint.

How can your pocket
be empty and still
have something in it?

*It can have
a hole in it.*

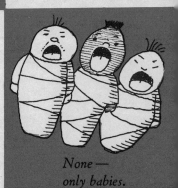

How many big men
have been born in
New York City?

*None —
only babies.*

ASTTCHNTMESAVESNNE

By inserting the letter I
four times above, what
well-known proverb is obtained?

A stitch in time saves nine.

Where do little dogs go when they are two years old?

Into their third year.

What can fill a whole barn and still weigh less than a handball?

Smoke.

What is the longest word in the English language?

SMILES. (There is a mile between the first and last letter.)

What number is
larger when you
turn it upside down?

6 becomes 9.

What runs around
the whole yard yet
never moves?

The fence.

Why is the letter U
never serious?

*It is always in
the midst of fun.*

What letter am I?

With me a word becomes a weapon.

With me age looks wise.

Add me to needles, and tailors
will moan.

S-word

S-age

needles-**S**

Do not put all your eggs
in one basket.

Where is a king crowned?

On the head.

When is a pig like ink?

*When it is
in a pen.*

Why does a good
resolution resemble
burnt toast?

*Because the
sooner it is
carried out,
the better.*

Where was Moses
when the light
went out?

In the dark.

2 many sp OIL s the

Too many cooks spoil the broth.

As round as an apple,
As deep as a cup,
And all the king's horses
Cannot pull it up.

> What is it?

/\\

In spring I look gay
Decked in comely array,
In summer more clothing I wear.
When colder it grows
I fling off my clothes,
And in winter quite naked appear.

> What am I?

A well.

∧∨∧∨∧∨∧∨∧∨∧∨∧∨∧∨∧∨∧∨∧∨∧∨∧∨

A tree.

East or West,
home is best.

Which burn longer: the candles on a
boy's birthday cake, or on a girl's?

TURN PAGE

75

They all burn shorter.

What has arms and
legs but no head?

A chair.

What belongs to you
but is used more often
by others?

Your name.

How can five persons
divide five eggs so
that each receives
one, and one still
remains in the dish?

*One person
takes the dish
with the egg.*

Little Nancy Etticoat
With a white petticoat
And a red nose;
She has no feet or hands;
The longer she stands,
The shorter she grows.

~~~~~~

As round as a pear,
As deep as a pail,
It never cries out
Though it's caught by the tail.

Candle in a
candlestick.

A bell.

I have to
work

because

paid
I am

*I have to
overwork
because
I am underpaid.*

How would you
describe this:
a HIbVE

*A small bee in
a big hive.*

What always has an
eye open but can't
see anything?

A needle.

Three men fell overboard but only
two got their hair wet. Why?

TURN PAGE

The third man was bald.

Look before you leap.

What has one foot
on each side and
one in the middle?

A yardstick.

How can you make
money fast?

*Glue it on
the wall.*

What is it that you
must keep after
giving it to someone
else?

Your word.

Stool — don't fall — stool

What does this mean?

Don't fall between two stools.

Why is a wild horse
like an egg?

*It must be
broken before
it can be used.*

Which month does
a soldier hate?

A long march.

When is coffee like
the surface of the
earth?

*When it is
ground.*

Why is a baby in the Bronx
brought up on elephant milk?

TURN PAGE

Because it is an elephant
baby in the Bronx Zoo.

What is less tired
the longer it runs?

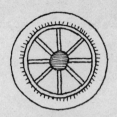

A wheel.

What is the number
which, if you divide
it, will leave you
nothing on either
side?

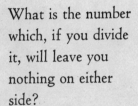

The number 8.

When Washington
crossed the Delaware,
what did he see on
his left hand?

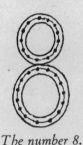

5 fingers.

What is the best thing
to make in a hurry?

Make haste.

Why are ghosts like
newspapers?

*Because they
appear in sheets.*

Why does a boy
envy a stamp?

*Because it can
be licked only
once.*

90

Why does a giraffe have such a
long neck?

TURN PAGE

*Because his head is so far
from his body.*

W **the** 🐱
is a 🏞️
the 🐭🐭 **will play**

When the cat is away
The mice will play.

I go, but never stir;
I run, but never walk;
I count, but never
    write;
I tell you much, but
    never talk.

What am I?

A clock.

Where were potatoes
first found?

In the ground.

Where did the Pilgrim Fathers stand
when they landed on Plymouth Rock?

TURN PAGE

On their feet.

Why is the letter T
like an island?

*Because it is in
the middle of
water.*

When is a trunk like
two letters in the
alphabet?

M T

*When it is M T
(empty).*

Why does a chicken
cross the road?

*To get to the
other side.*

What do you suppose
an envelope says when
it is licked?

*It shuts up and
says nothing.*

What question can
never be answered
by "Yes"?

"Are you asleep?"

Which moves faster —
heat or cold?

*Heat. (Everybody
can catch cold.)*

98

DON'T

DON'T
———
HEAR

Don't overhear.

DON'T
———
LOOK

Don't overlook.

DON'T
———
EAT

Don't overeat.

What has many leaves
but no stem?

A book.

What can be divided
by everyone, but
nobody can see where
it is divided?

Water.

Where do cherries
come from?

From a tree.

*Birds of a feather
flock together.*

My friend declared
that forty horses
have eighty-four legs.

How come?

*Forty horses
have eighty
forelegs.*

I show a different
face to everybody,
but have no face
myself.

What am I?

A mirror.

How is it that trees
put on their summer
dresses, without
opening their trunks?

*They leave
them out.*

What do hippopotamuses have that
no other animals have?

TURN PAGE

Little hippopotamuses.

What has four legs,
but only one foot?

A bed

What is the best way
to make a coat last?

*Make the pants
first.*

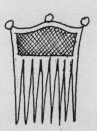

What has teeth but
can never eat?

A comb.

Which two letters creep up a wall?

Which two letters describe
a slippery sidewalk?

I — V   (ivy).

I — C   (icy).

What letter of
the alphabet is a
busy insect?

The letter B.

What fish does a girl
wear on her finger?

Her—ring.

Which side of an apple
is the left side?

*The part that
isn't eaten.*

Standing on a mountain top and looking through binoculars, what should you watch?

TURN PAGE

109

Your step.

What word can you
pronounce quicker
by adding a syllable
to it?

Quick.

Why does a baker
wear a big white hat?

*To keep his
head warm.*

Who was the heaviest
of inventors?

Fulton   (full—ton)

I am a tree without life or root,
Without a blossom, bud or flower,
Yet I have on my branches marvelous fruit
To delight you for many an hour.

What kind of tree am I?

Christmas tree.

If seven sisters
each has one brother,
how many children
are in the family?

Eight.

What is it that
has two heads,
six feet, one tail,
and four ears?

*It's you! —.when
you ride on a donkey.*

What day will be
yesterday and
was tomorrow?

Today.

What is filled every
morning and emptied
every night?

A shoe.

What starts with a T,
is full of T, and
ends with T?

A teapot.

What has five fingers
but neither flesh
nor bone?

A glove.

I hear you without
ears and answer you
without a mouth.

What am I?

Your echo.

Once in a minute
Twice in a moment.

What is it?

The letter M.

Tell me a word
to which you can add
a syllable and make
it still shorter.

Short.

Why is a policeman stronger
than the strongest man in the world?

TURN PAGE

*Because he can hold up
automobiles with one
hand.*

Why does a hen lay eggs?

*Because if she dropped them,
they would break.*

Paperbacks You'll Enjoy Anytime